A Magical Day in Sunnyside

Written by Amy Shoenthal
Illustrated by Kate Durkin

Archway Publishing books may be ordered through booksellers or by contacting:

Archway Publishing
1663 Liberty Drive
Bloomington, IN 47403
www.archwaypublishing.com
844-669-3957

ISBN: 978-1-6657-2426-5 (sc)
ISBN: 978-1-6657-2425-8 (e)

Print information available on the last page.

Archway Publishing rev. date: 07/19/2022

ARCHWAY
PUBLISHING

Cory Bea woke up one morning,
to a bright and sunny day.
She was so excited for
cousin Ava to come play!

She went to the door to greet her
and the girls bounded outside
to go explore the neighborhood—
New York City's Sunnyside.

Right by Cory's house
was a hundred-year-old tree.
At the bottom was a tiny door
which was sort of hard to see.

"The fairies who live down in there
will fly right through that door,
but only if we find their magic
hidden in a local store!"

The girls began their magic search,
the adventure would begin!
Their first stop: the coffee shop,
they smiled and walked in.

Liz made ice cream lattes
and Mary laughed along.
While music played around them,
they all danced and sang a song.

Just down Skillman Avenue
was another lovely spot.
It's a special yoga studio
that the locals love a lot.

"Namaste!" was Roque's greeting.
He rolled out mats with glee,
"There must be magic here,"
Ava said, posing like a tree.

SURYASIDE
yoga studio

"Perhaps there's magic in *this* store?"
Cory heard Ava say
as they browsed through all the records
and the lovely things at Stray.

Then Cory said to Ava,
"It's just past 10 o'clock!"
They turned on 49th Street,
and skipped right down the block.

"We're going to a place,
where the fun just never ends—
Sunnyside Gardens Park
where I play with all my friends!"

The girls rushed over to the gate
and once they were inside,
Lily and Ada greeted them
as Edmund slid down the slide.

Over in the sandbox,
Aaron's trucks were all the rage.
Nolan played some baseball
while Jackson grooved on the stage.

Jonah and Zayne waved hello
as they scooted right on by.
In the corner by the skate ramp
Mickey and Zora seemed to fly.

The picnic grove for lunch
is where all the friends did meet,
agreeing New York pizza
is the best you'll ever eat.

"There are more parks we can go to,"
Cory said out loud.
So they skipped on to Windmuller,
and peeked out at the crowd.

Runners jogging 'round the track,
and big kids playing ball,
the cousins went on stage
and performed a show for all!

From Cemitas el Tigre
to arepas on the street,
when you come on down to Sunnyside,
there's such good food to eat!

Cardamom has yummy saag.
Eat Ida's burgers in the back!
Or get Rica's pupusas
for a perfect midday snack.

The girls continued on their walk
and came upon a purple store,
with toys and gifts and lots of games,
plus clothes and shoes and more!

"We could all use a little magic,"
Violet said as they came in.
And she gave them each a fairy wand
as they browsed the toy bin.

"I forgot about our magic search!"
Ava said with delight.
And off to find that fairy,
the girls ran out of sight.

"There's a place I want to show you,"
Cory said, before dinnertime.
"You'll love Tangni and her flowers—
such bouquets you can design!"

Now with fairy wands and flowers
the girls walked around the bend.
They would find that fairy magic
as the day came to an end.

"Hello Belo!" Cory said,
as they were greeted at the door,
"More food?" Ava exclaimed,
"I think this is meal number four!"

"Of course," was Cory's answer,
as they ate salgados and fries.
"Sunnyside is just amazing!"
Ava shouted with surprise.

Just then Big Shane walked by
rolling his ice cream cart
and gave each girl delicious treats
before it was time to part.

The girls were full and sleepy
as they walked just one block more
and stopped at the big old tree
and its little fairy door.

They just could not believe it
as the small door opened wide!
And Rosie—a small fairy—
well, she flitted right outside!

"Your magic wands, they called me,
So I came to say hello.
I'm glad you had a lovely day
in this place that we love so."

And then the fairy, Rosie,
said goodbye and flew away.
Cory and Ava waved and smiled.
What a magical Sunnyside day!

Amy Shoenthal is a journalist and marketing executive whose work focuses on small businesses and entrepreneurs. As a contributor to ForbesWomen, she profiles today's most fascinating leaders, from startup founders to political leaders, celebrities and activists. Follow her @amysho on Instagram and Twitter.

Kate Durkin is an artist and illustrator who creates whimsical illustrations, paintings, and murals for kids and kids at heart. She's inspired by nature, food, her home in Sunnyside, Queens and her three children. Visit her online at katedurkinart.com.